Ca

Written by Jill Eggleton
Illustrated by Raymond McGrath

Rigby

The cake went
on the floor.

The hot dogs went on the floor.

The chips went
on the floor.

The pizzas went
on the floor.

A Menu

Party Food

 cake

 hot dogs

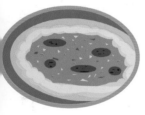 pizza

 chips

Guide Notes

Title: Cat Party
Stage: Emergent – Magenta

Genre: Fiction
Approach: Guided Reading
Processes: Thinking Critically, Exploring Language, Processing Information
Written and Visual Focus: Illustrative Text, Menu
Word Count: 37

FORMING THE FOUNDATION

Tell the children that the story is about a party and something that happens at a party. Talk to them about what is on the front cover. Read the title and the author/illustrator. "Walk" through the book, focusing on the illustrations and talking to the children about what is happening in each picture.
Leave pages 12-13 for prediction.

Read the text together.

THINKING CRITICALLY
(sample questions)

After the reading
- Why do you think the balloons popped?
- Look at pages 12-13. What do you think the kids will do now that all their party food is on the floor?

EXPLORING LANGUAGE
(ideas for selection)

Terminology
Title, cover, author, illustrator, illustrations

Vocabulary
Interest words: party, cake, pop, hot dogs, pizza, chips
High-frequency words: the, went, on, said
Positional word: on